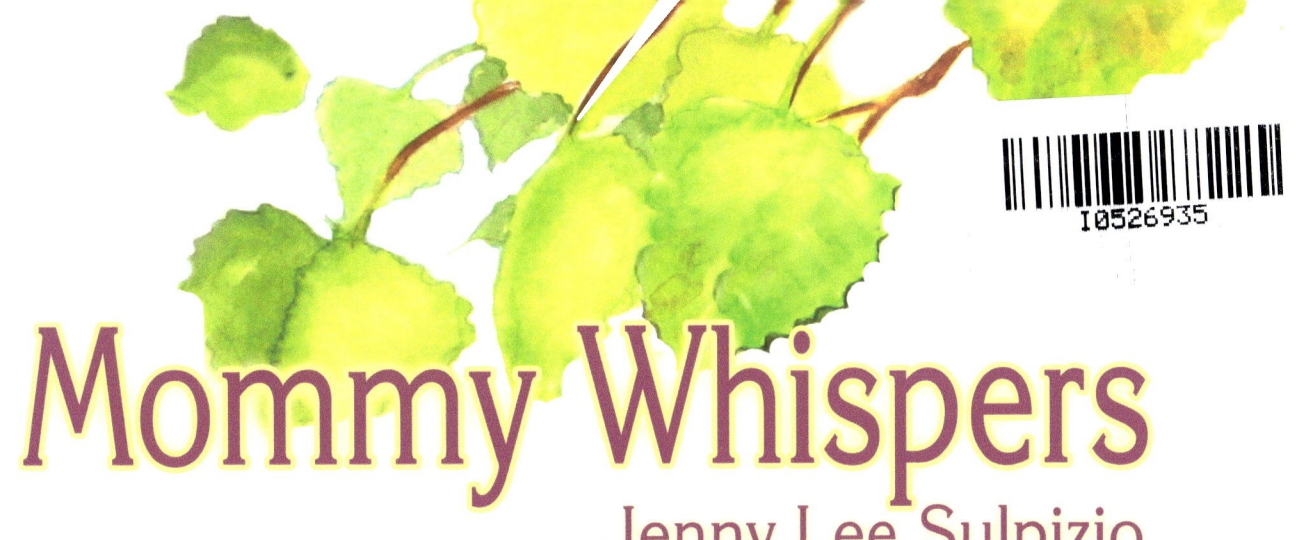

Mommy Whispers

Jenny Lee Sulpizio

Illustrated by Peg Lozier

Mommy Whispers

ISBN: 978-1-60920-013-8
Printed in the United States of America
©2010 by Jenny Lee Sulpizio
All rights reserved

Illustrations by Peg Lozier

Photos by
Laurie Brown Photography--Yuma, AZ
Tom Meinhold Photography--San Luis Obispo, CA

Layout and cover design by Ajoyin Publishing, Inc.

Library of Congress Cataloging-in-Publication Data

API
Ajoyin Publishing, Inc.
P.O. 342
Three Rivers, MI 49093
www.ajoyin.com

Please direct your inquiries to admin@ajoyin.com

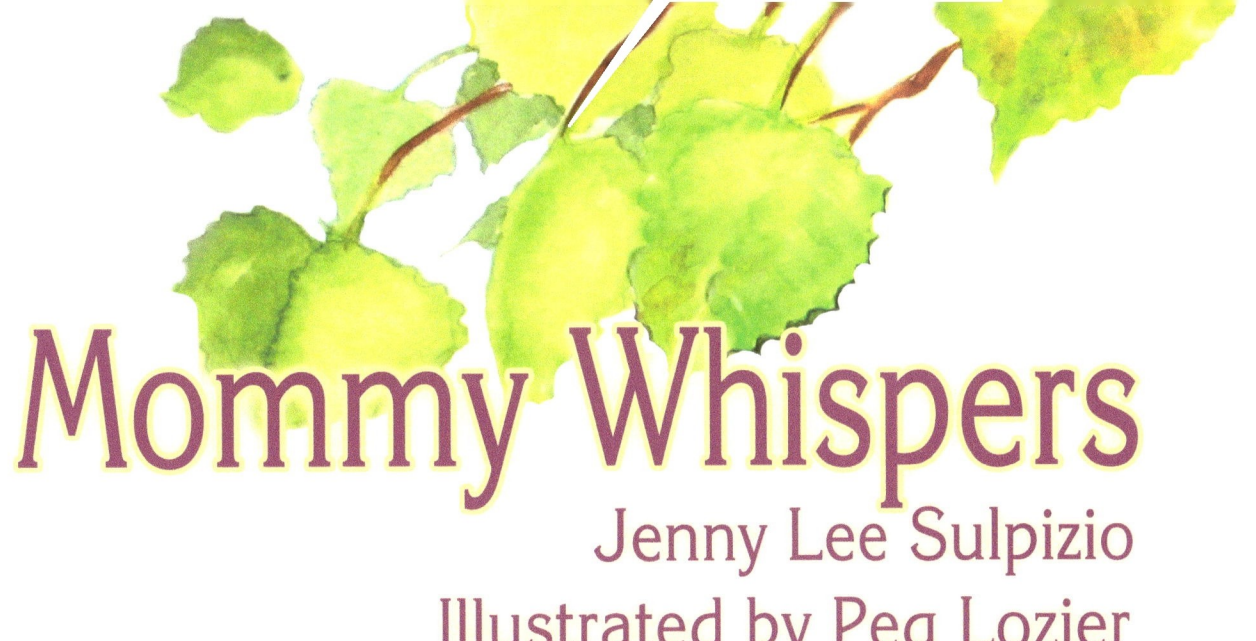

Mommy Whispers

Jenny Lee Sulpizio

Illustrated by Peg Lozier

JOYIN PUBLISHING INC.

http://www.ajoyin.com

Dedication

For Annie–I cherish the little girl you are and
look forward to seeing the woman you are to become.
As big as the world, as high as the sky, my love for you is unending...
In appreciation for God's gifts.
John 3:16
J.L.S

To George and Pat—my own parental units.

P.L.

My mother used to tell me that when I was a baby she would hold me close, rock me back and forth in her rocking chair, and sing to me over and over again. She would pray for my safety, for my health, and that God would help me grow into a woman sure of myself and my place in this world. She considered me a gift from above…a true miracle, and while I slept, she'd whisper in my little ear, **"You are God's gift to me, forever you will be,"** as I drifted off to dreamland.

When I grew into a toddler and began running around the house, the backyard, and all over the neighborhood, my mother told me that she would take a step back from the craziness, breathe in the moment and her surroundings, and pray that I would grow to be a woman who would never forget how to play hard or relinquish my zest for life. And as I ran all about, she'd chase after me, pull me close to her, and gently whisper, **"You are God's gift to me, forever you will be,"** as I broke away from her grasp and skipped down the street.

On the first day of kindergarten, when my excitement could hardly be contained--with new shoes and new clothes and all of my school supplies in tow, my mother knelt down and embraced me. She held on to me tight...not wanting to let go. And after a few moments, she began to pray that my school years would not go by in the blink of an eye, that I would develop a passion for learning and a determination to always do my best in every endeavor I undertook. And as she handed me my lunchbox and straightened my skirt, she gently whispered, **"You are God's gift to me, forever you will be,"** as I gave her a kiss and jumped on the school bus.

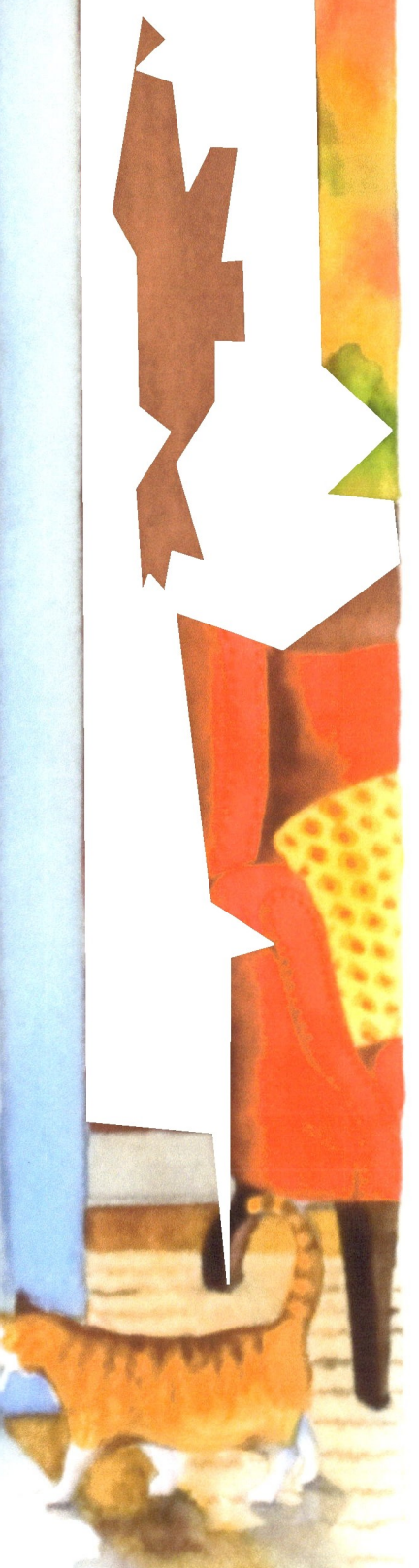

And when dolls and jump ropes were replaced by makeup and clothes, when I began noticing boys, and was in too much of a hurry to grow up, my mother would take time out to let me know that she would always have an ear to listen, to be there for me through the good times and the bad, through the heartaches and the pain. She would pray that I would grow to know the value and meaning of true and loyal friendships, and everlasting love.

She'd squeeze me tight and whisper, "**You are God's gift to me, forever you will be,**" as I ran out the door and off with my friends.

When the time came for me to move away from home and on to college…and after sensing the excitement over my newfound freedom, my mother held me close, and let me know how proud she was of the young woman I had become and the path I was taking. With a quivering voice she prayed that I would always know to follow my heart, and pray for strength and clarity whenever I was in doubt.

Backing out of the driveway,
with my car loaded down, she
walked up to the window and
whispered,
**"You are God's gift to me,
forever you will be,"** as
I pulled away from
the house and drove
off to school.

Years later, as I stood in a
beautiful white dress, preparing
to take my vows, my mother
was overcome by emotion.

Gone were the days of pigtails
and popsicles, car pools
and Girl Scouts…

I stood before her a woman representing the little girl she had to let go, and with tears in her eyes, she prayed that God would always be at the center of my marriage, my rock, and my refuge from the storms that would surely cross my path. She prayed that He would continue to bless me, watch over and protect me all the years of my life. And as she did so, she leaned over and gently whispered,

"You are God's gift to me, forever you will be," as she lowered my veil, and sent me down the aisle.

And as I prepared to enter motherhood, sensing my anxiousness, my mother told me that the greatest gift she ever received was the precious miracle of her baby girl. From the moment I was placed in her arms, she was filled with overwhelming emotion and appreciation of such an amazing blessing.

With her hand upon my belly,
she prayed for the life of my baby,
for the courage and wisdom it
would take to raise this child, and
for the ability to trust God and rely
on faith, no matter what was thrown
my way. And as she did so, she
gently whispered,

**"You are God's gift to me,
forever you will be,"** as my
unborn child kicked and kicked.

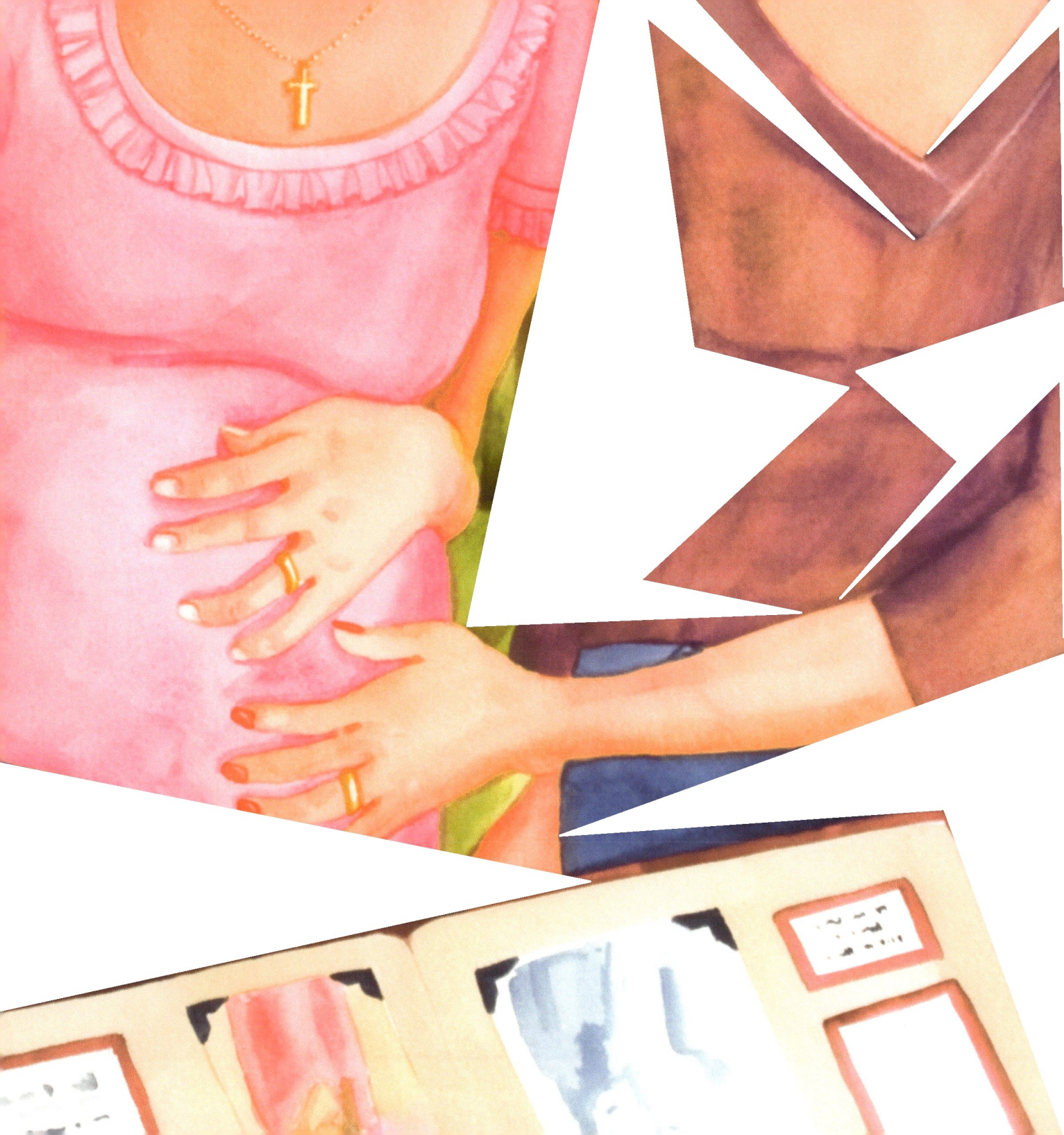

Gazing at my own newborn baby girl in all
her beauty, I couldn't help but thank God for
such a blessing. I immediately began to pray
for her safety, her health, and that He would
help her grow to become a woman sure of
herself and her place in this world.

As I held this precious gift, I prayed that I would become a mother much like my own, filled with love, compassion, and a deep and abiding faith. And as I prayed, I brought this new life to my lips and whispered in her tiny ear,

"You are God's gift to me, forever you will be," as she drifted off to dreamland.

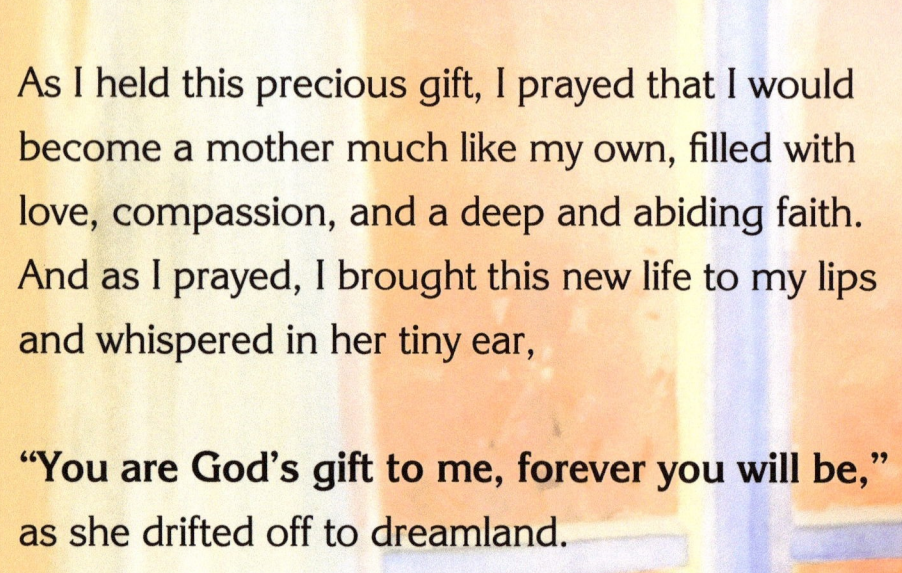

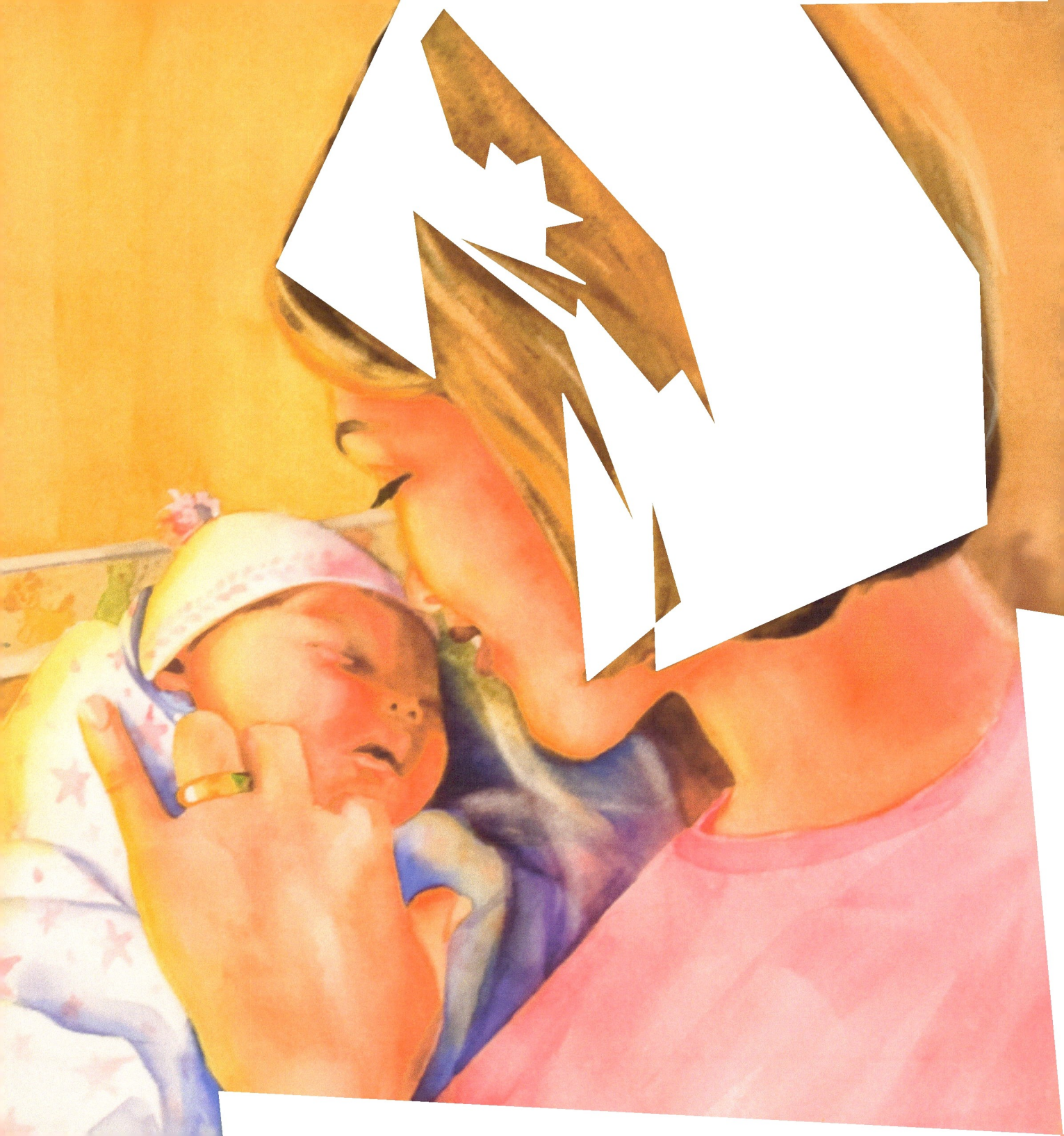

www.ingramcontent.com/pod-product-compliance
Lightning Source LLC
Chambersburg PA
CBHW041005170626
46815CB00002B/167